CHILDREN OF THE FUTURE

CHILDREN OF THE FUTURE

EDITED BY

Isaac Asimov
Martin Harry Greenberg
Charles Waugh

ILLUSTRATED BY

Joe Van Severen

RAINTREE PUBLISHERS
MILWAUKEE TORONTO MELBOURNE LONDON

ℬ BLACKWELL RAINTREE
OXFORD

Library of Congress Number: 83-21316

1 2 3 4 5 6 7 8 9 87 86 85 84

Printed and bound in the United States of America.

Library of Congress Cataloging in Publication Data

Main entry under title:

Children of the future.
  (Science fiction shorts)
    Contents: Introduction / Isaac Asimov—All summer in a day / Ray
Bradbury—Teething ring / James Causey—[etc.]
    1. Science fiction.   2. Children's stories.
[1. Science fiction.   2. Short stories]   I. Asimov, Isaac—1920-
II. Greenberg, Martin Harry.   III. Waugh, Charles.   IV. Van Severen,
Joe, ill.   V. Series.
PZ5.C4373   1984   [Fic]   83-21316
U.S. ISBN 0-8172-1740-1   (lib. bdg.)
U.K. SBN 0-86256-128-0

"All Summer in a Day" © 1954; copyright renewed © 1982 by Ray
    Bradbury. Reprinted by permission of Don Congdon
    Associates, Inc.
"Teething Ring" © 1952 by Galaxy Publishing Corporation.
    Reprinted by permission of the author.
"An End of Spinach" © 1981 by Mercury Press, Inc. From *The
    Magazine of Fantasy and Science Fiction*. Reprinted by
    permission of the author.
"The Boy Who Predicted Earthquakes" © 1950 by Margaret St.
    Clair. Copyright renewed © 1978 by Margaret St. Clair.
    Reprinted by permission of McIntosh and Otis, Inc.

Published simultaneously in the U.K. by Blackwell Raintree.

Contents

Introduction

ISAAC ASIMOV

We all know that the future is going to be different from today. The reason we know it is that for two centuries everything has been changing rapidly, mostly because of new inventions, and people have been watching that happen.

What's more, these changes have been coming faster and faster, so that even young people are aware of them.

Young people might not know that there was a time when there weren't any railroad trains or telegraphs or telephones unless they read about such times in history books. No one is old enough to have such times in their own memories. It even takes a very old person to remember when there weren't any airplanes, or radios.

However, I'm not very old and I can remember when there weren't any television sets or talking pictures. People considerably younger than I can remember when there weren't any color television sets or rockets to the moon. And even junior high school students can remember when there weren't any video games.

So we all know that things change.

Therefore, when we write stories about the future, we naturally picture societies that are quite different from our own. People will live in different kinds of houses, have different kinds of jobs, travel in different kinds of vehicles, have different ways of amusing themselves, and so on.

Just the same, science fiction stories are generally written by adults (sometimes rather aged adults like me) and, for some reason, adults usually (not always, but usually) write about adults. Sometimes it's possible to forget that children will also be living in the future and that their lives will be different, too. We just don't think about them, somehow, as often as we think of adults.

To see what I mean, pretend you had used a time machine to go a hundred years into the past and that you were trying to tell the people of the 1880s what life would be like in the 1980s. You might tell them a great many things about war weapons and jet planes and men on the moon, but what if they ask, "And what is it like for the children?"

Would you have remembered to tell them about comic books and movies and television and Disneyland and video games? Don't forget to tell them about schools because in those days very few children went to school for more than a few years, and they would be astonished to hear that in our own time, almost all children are expected to finish high school and that many of them go on to college. They would be even more astonished to find out that in the 1980s girls receive as much education as boys do. In the 1880s, that certaintly wasn't true.

There might be some other good news you would have to tell them. In the 1880s, for instance, there were many child-ren's diseases that were highly dangerous and often fatal. In the 1980s, on the other hand, there are all kinds of "shots" that children are given to make them immune to certain diseases. There are also antibiotics that can cure diseases that children do get. We know about vitamins that help children avoid being malnourished. As a result, far fewer children die of disease now than then.

There is some bad news, too, of course. There are drug problems that we have now that didn't exist a hundred years ago. And of course children can die in automobile accidents or in plane crashes, and this never happened in the days when there were no automobiles or airplanes.

So we can look forward to a future in which, perhaps, children might have different amusements on different planets, or different abilities, or undergo different dangers. It makes for interesting stories.

All Summer in a Day

RAY BRADBURY

"Ready?"

"Ready."

"Now?"

"Soon."

"Do the scientists really know? Will it happen today, will it?"

"Look, look; see for yourself!"

The children pressed to each other like so many roses, so many weeds, intermixed, peering out for a look at the hidden sun.

It rained.

It had been raining for seven years; thousands upon thousands of days compounded and filled from one end to the other with rain, with the drum and gush of water, with the sweet crystal fall of showers and the concussion of storms so heavy they were tidal waves come over the islands. A thousand forests had been crushed under the rain and grown up a thousand times to be crushed again. And this was the way life was forever on the planet Venus, and this was the school room of the children of the rocket men and women who had come to a raining world to set up civilization and live out their lives.

"It's stopping, it's stopping!"

"Yes, yes!"

Margot stood apart from them, from these children who could never remember a time when there wasn't rain and rain and rain. They were all nine years old, and if there had been a day, seven years ago, when the sun came out for an hour and showed its face to the stunned world, they could not recall. Sometimes, at night, she heard them stir, in remembrance, and she knew they were dreaming and remembering gold or a yellow crayon or a coin large enough to buy the world with. She knew that they thought they remembered a warmness, like a blushing in the face, in the body, in the arms and legs and trembling hands. But then they always awoke to the tatting drum, the endless shaking down of clear bead necklaces upon the roof, the walk, the gardens, the forest, and their dreams were gone.

All day yesterday they had read in class, about the sun. About how like a lemon it was, and how hot. And they had written small stories or essays or poems about it:

> I think the sun is a flower,
> That blooms for just one hour.

That was Margot's poem, read in a quiet voice in the still classroom while the rain was falling outside.

"Aw, you didn't write that!" protested one of the boys.

"I did," said Margot. "I *did*."

"William!" said the teacher.

But that was yesterday. Now, the rain was slackening, and the children were crushed to the great thick windows.

"Where's teacher?"

"She'll be back."

"She'd better hurry, we'll miss it!"

They turned on themselves, like a feverish wheel, all tumbling spokes.

Margot stood alone. She was a very frail girl who looked as if she had been lost in the rain for years and the rain had washed out the blue from her eyes and the red from her mouth and the yellow from her hair. She was an old photograph dusted from an album, whitened away, and if she spoke at all her voice would be a ghost. Now she stood, separate, staring at the rain and the loud wet world beyond the huge glass.

"What're *you* looking at?" said William.

Margot said nothing.

"Speak when you're spoken to." He gave her a shove. But she

did not move; rather, she let herself be moved only by him and nothing else.

They edged away from her, they would not look at her. She felt them go away. And this was because she would play no games with them in the echoing tunnels of the underground city. If they tagged her and ran, she stood blinking after them and did not follow. When the class sang songs about happiness and life and games, her lips barely moved. Only when they sang about the sun and the summer did her lips move, as she watched the drenched windows.

And then, of course, the biggest crime of all was that she had come here only five years ago from Earth, and she remembered the sun and the way the sun was and the sky was, when she was four, in Ohio. And they, they had been on Venus all their lives, and they had been only two years old when last the sun came out, and had long since forgotten the color and heat of it and the way that it really was. But Margot remembered.

"It's like a penny," she said, once, eyes closed.

"No it's not!" the children cried.

"It's like a fire," she said, "in the stove."

"You're lying, you don't remember!" cried the children.

But she remembered and stood quietly apart from all of them, and watched the patterning windows. And once, a month ago, she had refused to shower in the school shower-rooms, had clutched her hands to her ears and over her head, screaming the water mustn't touch her head. So after that, dimly, dimly, she sensed it, she was different and they knew her difference and kept away.

There was talk that her father and mother were taking her back to Earth next year; it seemed vital to her that they do so, though it would mean the loss of thousands of dollars to her family. And so the children hated her for all these reasons, of big and little consequence. They hated her pale snow face, her waiting silence, her thinness and her possible future.

"Get away!" The boy gave her another push. "What're you waiting for?"

Then, for the first time, she turned and looked at him. And what she was waiting for was in her eyes.

"Well, don't wait around here!" cried the boy, savagely. "You won't see nothing!"

Her lips moved.

"Nothing!" he cried. "It was all a joke, wasn't it?" He turned to the other children. "Nothing's happening today. *Is* it?"

They all blinked at him and then, understanding, laughed and shook their heads. "Nothing, nothing!"

"Oh, but," Margot whispered, her eyes helpless. "But this is the day, the scientists predict, they say, they *know*, the sun . . ."

"All a joke!" said the boy, and seized her roughly. "Hey, everyone, let's put her in a closet before teacher comes!"

"No," said Margot, falling back.

They surged about her, caught her up and bore her, protesting, and then pleading, and then crying, back into a tunnel, a room, a closet, where they slammed and locked the door. They stood looking at the door and saw it tremble from her beating and throwing herself against it. They heard her muffled cries. Then, smiling, they turned and went out and back down the tunnel, just as the teacher arrived.

"Ready, children?" She glanced at her watch.

"Yes!" said everyone.

"Are we all here?"

"Yes!"

The rain slackened still more.

They crowded to the huge door.

The rain stopped.

It was as if, in the midst of a film concerning an avalanche, a tornado, a hurricane, a volcanic eruption, something had, first, gone wrong with the sound apparatus, thus muffling and finally cutting off all noise, all of the blasts and repercussions and thunders, and then, secondly, ripped the film from the projector and inserted in its place a peaceful tropical slide which did not move or tremor. The world ground to a standstill. The silence was so immense and unbelievable that you felt that your ears had been stuffed or you had lost your hearing altogether. The children put their hands to their ears. They stood apart. The door slid back and the smell of the silent, waiting world came in to them.

The sun came out.

It was the color of flaming bronze and it was very large. And the sky around it was a blazing blue tile color. And the jungle burned with sunlight as the children, released from their spell, rushed out, yelling into the summer-time.

"Now, don't go too far," called the teacher after them. "You've only one hour, you know. You wouldn't want to get caught out!"

But they were running and turning their faces up to the sky and feeling the sun on their cheeks like a warm iron; they were taking off their jackets and letting the sun burn their arms.

"Oh, it's better than the sun-lamps, isn't it?"

"Much, much better!"

They stopped running and stood in the great jungle that covered Venus, that grew and never stopped growing, tumultuously, even as you watched it. It was a nest of octopuses, clustering up great arms of fleshlike weed, wavering, flowering in this brief spring. It was the color of rubber and ash, this jungle, from the many years without sun. It was the color of stones and white cheeses and ink.

The children lay out, laughing, on the jungle mattress, and heard it sigh and squeak under them, resilient and alive. They ran among the trees, they slipped and fell, they pushed each other, they played hide-and-seek and tag, but most of all they squinted at the sun until tears ran down their faces, they put their hands up at that yellowness and that amazing blueness and they breathed of the fresh fresh air and listened and listened to the silence which suspended them in a blessed sea of no sound and no motion. They looked at everything and savored everything. Then, wildly, like animals escaped from their caves, they ran and ran in shouting circles. They ran for an hour and did not stop running.

And then—

In the midst of their running, one of the girls wailed.

Everyone stopped.

The girl, standing in the open, held out her hand.

"Oh, look, look," she said, trembling.

They came slowly to look at her opened palm.

In the center of it, cupped and huge, was a single raindrop.

She began to cry, looking at it.

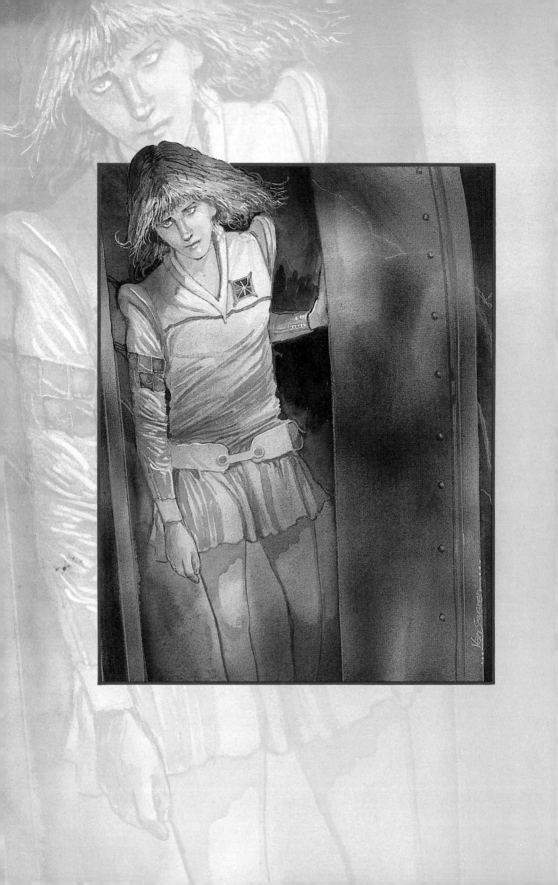

They glanced quickly at the sky.

"Oh. Oh."

A few cold drops fell on their noses and their cheeks and their mouths. The sun faded behind a stir of mist. A wind blew cool around them. They turned and started to walk back toward the underground house, their hands at their sides, their smiles vanishing away.

A boom of thunder startled them and like leaves before a new hurricane, they tumbled upon each other and ran. Lightning struck ten miles away, five miles away, a mile, a half-mile. The sky darkened into midnight in a flash.

They stood in the doorway of the underground house for a moment until it was raining hard. Then they closed the door and heard the gigantic sound of the rain falling in tons and avalanches everywhere and forever.

"Will it be seven more years?"

"Yes. Seven."

Then one of them gave a little cry.

"Margot!"

"She's still in the closet where we locked her."

"Margot."

They stood as if someone had driven them, like so many stakes, into the floor. They looked at each other and then looked away. They glanced out at the world that was raining now and raining and raining steadily. They could not meet each other's glances. Their faces were solemn and pale. They looked at their hands and feet, their faces down.

"Margot."

One of the girls said, "Well . . . ?"

No one moved.

"Go on," whispered the girl.

They walked slowly down the hall in the sound of cold rain. They turned through the doorway to the room, in the sound of the storm and thunder, lightning on their faces, blue and terrible. They walked over to the closet door slowly and stood by it.

Behind the closet door was only silence.

They unlocked the door, even more slowly, and let Margot out.

Teething Ring

JAMES CAUSEY

Half an hour before, while she had been engrossed in the current soap opera and Harry Junior was screaming in his crib, Melinda would naturally have slammed the front door in the little man's face. However, when the bell rang, she was wearing her new Chinese-red housecoat, had just lustered her nails to a blinding scarlet, and Harry Junior was sleeping like an angel.

Yawning, Melinda answered the door and the little man said, beaming, "Excellent day. I have geegaws for information."

Melinda did not quite recoil. He was perhaps five feet tall, with a gleaming hairless scalp and a young-old face. He wore a plain gray tunic, and a peddler's tray hung from his thin shoulders.

"Don't want any," Melinda stated flaty.

"Please." He had great, beseeching amber eyes. "They all say that. I haven't much time. I must be back at the university by noon."

"You working your way through college?"

He brightened. "Yes. I suppose you could call it that. Alien anthropology major."

Melinda softened.

"Well?" she asked grudgingly. "What's in the tray?"

"Flangers," said the little man eagerly. "Oscilloscopes. Portable force field generators. A neural distorter." Melinda's face was blank. The little man frowned."You use them, of course? This *is* a Class IV culture?" Melinda essayed a weak shrug, and the little man sighed with relief. His eyes fled past her to the blank screen of the TV set. "Ah, a monitor." He smiled. "For a moment I was afraid—may I come in?"

Melinda shrugged, opened the door. This might be interesting, like a vacuum-cleaner salesman who had cleaned her drapes last week for free. And *Kitty Kyle Battles Life* wouldn't be on for almost an hour.

"My name is Porteous," said the little man with an eager smile. "I'm doing a thematic on Class IV cultures." He whipped out a stylus, began jotting down notes. The TV set fascinated him.

"It's turned off right now," Melinda said.

Porteous's eyes widened impossibly. "You mean," he whispered in horror, "that you're exercising Class V privileges? This is terribly confusing. I get doors slammed in my face, when Class IV's are supposed to have a splendid gregarian quotient—you *do* have atomic power, don't you?"

"Oh, sure," said Melinda uncomfortably.

"Space travel?" The little face was intent, sharp.

"Well," Melinda yawned, looking at the blank screen, "They've got *Space Patrol, Space Cadet, Tales of Tomorrow...*"

"Excellent. Rocket ships or force fields?" Melinda blinked. "Does your husband own one?" Melinda shook her head helplessly. "What are your economic circumstances?"

Melinda took a deep rasping breath, said, "Listen, mister, is this a demonstration or a quiz program?"

"Oh, my excuse. Demonstration, certainly. You will not mind the questions?"

"Questions?" There was an ominous glint in Melinda's blue eyes.

"Your delightful primitive customs, art forms, personal habits—"

"Look," Melinda said, crimsoning. "This is a respectable neighborhood, and I'm not answering any Kinsey report, understand?"

The little man nodded, scribbling. "Personal habits are taboo? I so regret. The demonstration." He waved grandly at the tray. "Anti-grav sandals? A portable solar converter? Apologizing for this miserable selection, but on Capella they told me—" He followed Melinda's entranced gaze, selected a tiny green vial. "This is merely a regenerative solution. You appear to have no cuts or bruises."

"Oh," said Melinda nastily. "Cures warts, cancer, grows hair, I suppose."

Porteous brightened. "Of course. I see you scan. Amazing." He scribbled further with his stylus, glanced up, blinked at the obvious scorn on Melinda's face. "Here. Try it."

"You try it." Now watch him squirm!

Porteous hesitated. "Would you like me to grow an extra finger, hair—"

"Grow some hair." Melinda tried not to smile.

The little man unstopped the vial, poured a shimmering green drop on his wrist, frowning.

Melinda's jaw dropped. She stared at the tiny tuft of hair which had sprouted on that bare wrist. She was thinking abruptly, unhappily, about that chignon she had bought yesterday. They had let her buy that for eight dollars when with this stuff she could have a natural one.

"How much?" she inquired cautiously.

"A half-hour of your time only," said Porteous.

"Okay, shoot. But nothing personal."

Porteous was delighted. He asked a multitude of questions, most of them pointless, some naive, and Melinda dug into her infinitesimal fund of knowledge and gave.

"You mean," he asked in amazement, "that you live in these primitive huts of your own volition?"

"It's a GI housing project," Melinda said, ashamed.

"Astonishing." He wrote: *Feudal anachronisms and atomic power, side by side. Class IV's periodically "rough it" in back-to-nature movements.*

Harry Junior chose that moment to begin screaming for his lunch. Porteous sat, trembling "Is that a security alarm?"

"My son," said Melinda despondently, and she went into the nursery.

Porteous followed, and watched the ululating child with some trepidation. "Newborn?"

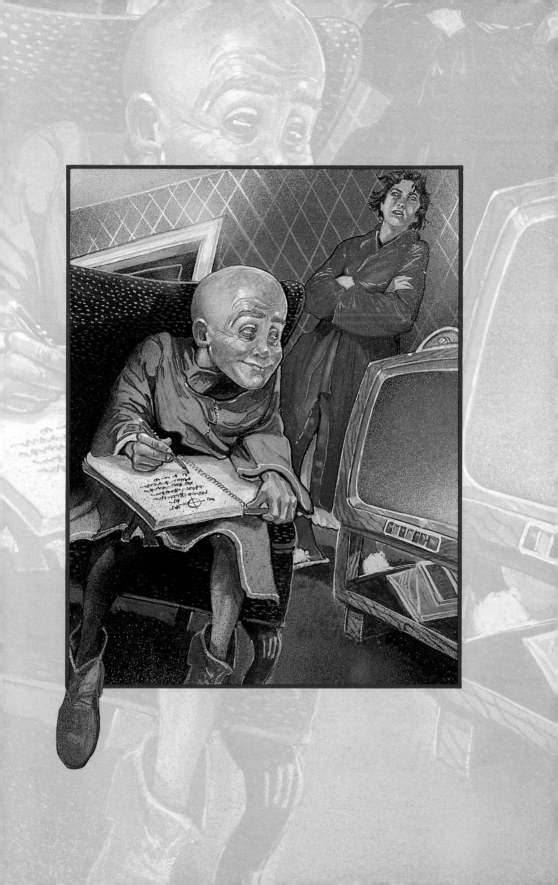

"Eighteen months," said Melinda stiffly, changing diapers. "He's cutting teeth."

Porteous shuddered. "What a pity. Obviously atavistic. Wouldn't the crèche accept him? You shouldn't have to keep him here."

"I keep after Harry to get a maid, but he says we can't afford one."

"Manifestly insecure," muttered the little man, studying Harry Junior. "Definite paranoid tendencies."

"He was two weeks premature," volunteered Melinda. "He's real sensitive."

"I know just the thing," Porteous said happily. "Here." He dipped into the glittering litter on the tray and handed Harry Junior a translucent prism. "A neural distorter. We use it to train regressives on Rigel Two. It might be of assistance."

Melinda eyed the thing doubtfully. Harry Junior was peering into the shifting crystal depths with a somewhat strained expression.

"Speeds up the neural flow," explained the little man proudly. "Helps tap the unused eighty per cent. The presymptomatic memory is unaffected because of automatic cerebral lapse in case of overload. I'm afraid it won't do much more than cube his present IQ, and an intelligent idiot is still an idiot, but—"

"How dare you?" Melinda's eyes flashed. "My son is *not* an idiot! You get out of here this minute and take your . . . things with you." As she reached for the prism, Harry Junior squalled. Melinda relented. "Here," she said angrily, fumbling with her purse. "How much are they?"

"Medium of exchange?" Porteous rubbed his bald skull. "Oh, I really shouldn't—but it'll make such a wonderful addendum to the chapter on malignant primitives. What is your smallest demonination?"

"Is a dollar okay?" Melinda was hopeful.

Porteous was pleased with the picture of George Washington. He turned the bill over and over in his fingers, at last bowed low and formally, apologized for any taboo violations and left via the front door.

"Crazy fraternities," muttered Melinda, turning on the TV.

Kitty Kyle was dull that morning. At length Melinda used some of the liquid in the green vial on her eyelashes, was quite pleased at the results, and hid the rest in the medicine cabinet.

Harry Junior was a model of docility the rest of that day. While Melinda watched TV and munched chocolates, did and re-did her hair, Harry Junior played quietly with the crystal prism.

Toward late afternoon, he crawled over to the bookcase, wrestled down the encyclopedia and pawed through it, gurgling with delight. He definitely, Melinda decided, would make a fine lawyer someday, not a useless putterer like Big Harry, who worked all hours overtime in that lab. She scowled as Harry Junior, bored with the encyclopedia, began reaching for one of Big Harry's tomes on nuclear physics. One putterer in the family was enough! But when she tried to take the book away from him, Harry Junior howled so violently that she let well enough alone.

At six-thirty, Big Harry called from the lab, with the usual despondent message that he would not be home for supper. Melinda said a few resigned things about cheerless dinners eaten alone, and Harry said he was very sorry but this might be *it*, and Melinda hung up on him in a temper.

Precisely fifteen minutes later, the doorbell rang. Melinda opened the front door and gaped. This little man could have been Porteous's double, except for the black metallic tunic, the glacial gray eyes.

"Mrs. Melinda Adams?" Even the voice was frigid.

"Y-Yes. Why—"

"Major Nord, Galactic Security." The little man bowed. "You were visited early this morning by one Porteous." He spoke the name with a certain disgust. "He left a neural distorter here. Correct?"

Melinda's nod was tremulous. Major Nord came quietly into the living room, shut the door behind him. "My apologies, madam, for the intrusion. Porteous mistook your world for a Class IV culture, instead of a Class VII. Here—" He handed her the crumpled dollar bill. "You may check the serial number. The distorter, please."

Melinda shrunk limply onto the sofa. "I don't understand," she said painfully. "Was he a thief?"

"He was . . . careless about his spatial coordinates." Major Nord's teeth showed in the faintest of smiles. "He has been corrected. Where is it?"

"Now look," said Melinda with some asperity. "That thing's kept Harry Junior quiet all day. I bought it in good faith, and it's not my fault—say, have you got a warrant?"

"Madam," said the Major with dignity, "I dislike violating local taboos, but must I explain the impact of a neural distorter on a backwater culture? What if your Neanderthal had been given atomic blasters? Where would *you* have been today? Swinging through the trees, no doubt. What if your Hitler had force fields?" He exhaled. "Where is your son?"

In the nursery, Harry Junior was contentedly playing with his blocks. The prism lay glinting in the corner.

Major Nord picked it up carefully, scrutinized Harry Junior. His voice was very soft.

"You said he was . . . playing with it?"

Some vestigial maternal instinct prompted Melinda to shake her head vigorously. The little man stared hard at Harry Junior, who began whimpering. Trembling, Melinda scooped up Harry Junior.

"Is *that* all you have to do—run around frightening women and children? Take your old distorter and get out. Leave decent people alone!"

Major Nord frowned. If only he could be sure. He peered stonily at Harry Junior, murmured, "Definite egomania. It doesn't seem to have affected him. Strange."

"Do you want me to scream?" Melinda demanded.

Major Nord sighed. He bowed to Melinda, went out, closed the door, touched a tiny stud on his tunic, and vanished.

"The manners of some people," Melinda said to Harry Junior. She was relieved that the Major had not asked for the green vial.

Harry Junior also looked relieved, although for quite a different reason.

Big Harry arrived home a little after eleven. There were small worry creases about his mouth and forehead, and the leaden

cast of defeat in his eyes. He went into the bedroom, and Melinda sleepily told him about the little man working his way through college by peddling silly goods and about that rude cop named Nord. Harry said that was simply astonishing.

But Harry wanted to talk about work. "You married a failure, dear. Part of the experimental model vaporized, *wooosh*, just like that. On paper it looked so good—"

Melinda had heard it all before. She asked him to see if Harry Junior was covered, and Big Harry went unsteadily into the nursery, sat down by his son's crib.

"Poor little guy," he mused. "Your old man's a bum, a useless tinker. He thought he could send Man to the stars on a string of helium nuclei. Oh, he was smart. Thought of everything. Auxiliary jets to kick off the negative charge, bigger mercury vapor banks—a fine straight thrust of positive alpha particles." He hiccuped, put his face to his hands.

"Didn't you ever stop to think that a few air molecules could defocus the stream? Try a vacuum, stupid."

Big Harry stood up.

"Did you say something son?"

"Gurfle," said Harry Junior.

Big Harry reeled into the living room like a somnambulist.

He got pencil and paper, began jotting frantic formulae. Presently he called a cab and raced back to the laboratory.

Melinda was dreaming about little bald men with diamond-studded trays. They were chasing her, they kept pelting her with rubies and emeralds, all they wanted was to ask questions, but she kept running, Harry Junior clasped tightly in her arms. Now they were ringing alarm bells. The bells kept ringing and she groaned, sat up in bed, and seized the telephone.

"Darling." Big Harry's voice shook. "I've got it! More auxiliary shielding plus a vacuum. We'll be rich!"

"That's just fine," said Melinda crossly. "You woke the baby."

Harry Junior was sobbing bitterly into his pillow. He was sick with disappointment. Even the most favorable extrapolation showed it would take him nineteen years to become master of the world.

An eternity. Nineteen years!

An End of Spinach

STAN DRYER

"Hey, Harry, I don't think we should be in here."

"Cummon, Spike, my Dad lets me come in here all the time and watch him."

"I know, but suppose he finds out we're here?"

"He won't know. See that TV monitor there? That shows the corridor outside his office so we can see him coming. Besides, we're not going to hurt anything, just talk to old Socrat a little."

"Talk to Socrat?"

"Socrat, the computer, dummy. That's what my Dad does all the time. You just type in the entry code on this terminal. I'll show you. 'LOGON PEMBROKE.'"

"PLEASE ENTER YOUR PASSWORD AT THE TERMINAL."

"Harry, it spoke *out loud* to us!"

"Of course. Now I'll type the password. 'MARS.' That's what Dad used the last time."

"ENTERED PASSWORD WAS ILLEGAL."

"See, Harry, I knew you weren't supposed to use it."

"Don't be dumb, Spike. They just change the password every month. I bet my Dad uses the names of the planets starting with the Sun and working out. Let me try the next one beyond Mars. 'JUPITER.'"

"ENTERED PASSWORD WAS ILLEGAL. IF ANOTHER ILLEGAL PASSWORD IS ENTERED, AN UNAUTORIZED ENTRY ALARM WILL BE GENERATED."

"Let's get out of here, Harry! You give it another bad password and it will ring a bell or lock the door on us!"

"Look, Spike, I know my Dad. He probably started with the names of the planets on the *outside* of the solar system and worked in. Watch this. I'll type 'EARTH.'"

"GOOD AFTERNOON, PROFESSOR PEMBROKE. SOCRAT AT YOUR SERVICE. AUDIBLE INPUTS MAY BE USED."

"Wow, Harry, you did it. It thinks it's talking to your Dad."

"I told you it was easy. Now what shall we ask it to do?"

"I CANNOT PARSE YOUR AUDIBLE INPUTS. PLEASE SPEAK MORE CLEARLY."

"I was just talking to my friend Spike. Let's see. To start, can you tell us what day it is today?"

"TODAY IS TUESDAY, MAY TWELVE, NINETEEN EIGHTY-SEVEN."

"Gee, Harry, that's neat. Can it do math stuff too?"

"Sure, watch this. Socrat, what is the square root of two?"

"TO HOW MANY DECIMAL PLACES DO YOU WISH THE SQUARE ROOT OF TWO CALCULATED?"

"How about a hundred?"

"THE SQUARE ROOT OF TWO TO ONE HUNDRED DECIMAL PLACES IS DISPLAYED ON SCREEN A."

"Look at that, Harry! It didn't take any time at all. One point four one four two one. . . . You think it's right?"

"Of course it's right. But we'll have Socrat check it for us. Watch this. Hey, Socrat, I want you to multiply the number on Screen A by itself."

"THE VALUE OF THE PRODUCT OF THE NUMBER ON SCREEN AND THE NUMBER ON SCREEN A IS DISPLAYED ON SCREEN B."

"There it is, Harry, a two followed by about a hundred zeroes. Hey, do you think Socrat could figure out the square root of two to a really big number of decimal places?"

"I'll ask it. Socrat, to how many decimal places can you find out the square root of two?"

"CALCULATIONS OF ROOTS OF NUMBERS ARE LIMITED ONLY BY THE MACHINE RESOURCES YOU WISH TO DEVOTE TO THE PROBLEM AND THE TIME YOU ARE WILLING TO WAIT FOR RESULTS."

"Okay, Socrat, how long would it take to get it to a million decimal places?"

"BY DEVOTING FULL CAPACITY OF THIS MACHINE TO THE TASK, IT COULD BE COMPLETED IN THIRTY-SEVEN SECONDS. WHERE DO YOU WISH YOUR OUTPUT PLACED?"

"Can I get it printed?"

"AFFIRMATIVE. PRINTOUT OF ONE MILLION DIGITS WILL REQUIRE SEVEN POINT SIX MINUTES. DO YOU WISH ME TO PERFORM THE CALCULATION?"

"What do you think, Spike?"

"Wait, Harry. Ask it how long it will take to get to a hundred billion decimal places."

"A hundred billion?"

"Sure. I bet it can't do that."

"I bet it can. Socrat, how long will it take you to figure out the square root of two to a hundred billion places?"

"BY DEVOTING THE FULL CAPACITY OF THIS MACHINE TO THAT TASK, THE SQUARE ROOT OF TWO COULD BE CALCULATED TO TEN TO THE ELEVENTH DECIMAL PLACES IN APPROXIMATELY FORTY-THREE DAYS AND SEVEN HOURS. PRINTOUT OF THE RESULTS WOULD REQUIRE FIVE HUNDRED AND TWENTY-EIGHT DAYS."

"See, Harry, I knew it couldn't do it."

"Hold on, Spike. I haven't finished asking it. First of all, Socrat, what can you do with the output if you don't print it?"

"OUTPUT CAN BE STORED ON DISK MEMORY FOR RECALL TO SCREEN DISPLAY AS REQUIRED. REQUISITE DISK STORAGE IS NOT CURRENTLY AVAILABLE."

"I told you it couldn't do it."

"Just hang on, Spike. Socrat, is there anything you could erase from the disk storage to make room?"

"AS A PRIORITY-ONE USER, YOU HAVE AUTHORIZATION TO ERASE ANY CURRENT FILES. STORAGE OF TEN TO THE ELEVENTH POWER DIGITS WILL REQUIRE APPROXIMATELY NINETY-THREE PERCENT OF ONLINE DISK PACK STORAGE AT THIS FACILITY. DO YOU WISH ME TO ERASE THIS STORAGE?"

"Not yet. We can't wait forty-three days to get the answer. Are there any other computers you can get to help with the job?"

"AS A PRIORITY-ONE USER YOU HAVE ACCESS TO ALL OTHER MACHINES ON THE NETWORK AND CAN EXECUTE AT PRIORITY ONE ON ALL SUCH MACHINES. THREE HUNDRED AND SIXTY-EIGHT MACHINES ARE CURRENTLY ON LINE.."

"If we used all of them, how long would it take?"

"UTILIZATION OF THE FULL FACILITIES OF ALL MACHINES CURRENTLY ON LINE WOULD REDUCE CALCULATION TIME TO APPROXIMATELY SEVENTEEN HOURS AND TWELVE MINUTES."

"Hey, Harry, that's great. We could turn all the computers loose right now and then come back after school tomorrow and look at the answer."

"Just a second, Spike. I'm not sure that's a good idea."

"How come?"

"Look, if we erase all the disk files here and stop all those other computers so they can do our stuff, someone's going to notice. Besides, Socrat might be doing something important he shouldn't stop doing."

"I thought Socrat was talking to us."

"You dummy. Socrat can talk to us and do a hundred other things at the same time."

"Go on, Harry. You're kidding me."

"I'm not. I'll ask it what it's doing. Hey, Socrat, what important things are you doing right now?"

"I CANNOT INDEX ON THE WORD 'IMPORTANT.' JOBS ARE CATEGORIZED BY PRIORITY AND USER.."

"Okay, give me a list of all the Priority-One jobs you're doing right now."

"LISTING OF PRIORITY-ONE JOBS DISPLAYED ON SCREEN A."

"Hey, look at that, Harry. That satellite catalog looks pretty interesting. Maybe we could print out a list of them?"

"Naw, Spike, you can get that stuff in a science book. Dad is always talking about his Land Use Planning Program. Let's mess around with that."

"What's it do?"

"Socrat, tell us about the Land Use Planning Program."

"THE LAND USE PLANNING PROGRAM AUTOMATES THE PROCESS OF DETERMINATION OF PRIORITIES FOR LAND USE FOR AGRICULTURE IN THE UNITED STATES. IT MATCHES REQUIREMENTS FOR FOOD PRODUCTS AGAINST AVAILABLE LAND. OUTPUT IS PROVIDED TO FIFTY-SEVEN REGIONAL PLANNING CENTERS WHERE FARMERS CAN OBTAIN PERTINENT INFORMATION OF CROP REQUIREMENTS."

"Spike, I got a great idea! What's your least favorite vegetable?"

"That's easy. Spinach."

"Mine too. Now what's your *favorite* vegetable?"

"Peas, I guess. How come you want to know that?"

"My idea, stupid. We're going to have Socrat stop everyone from growing spinach and have them grow lots more peas."

"Wow, Harry, neat."

"Socrat, how much spinach is grown in the United States every year?"

"ONE HUNDRED AND NINETY-EIGHT THOUSAND SHORT TONS OF SPINACH WERE GROWN IN THE UNITED STATES DURING THE LAST PLANNING YEAR."

"Okay, can you set it so no more spinach is grown from now on?"

"NEGATIVE. CHANGES IN CROP ACREAGE ALLOCATION ARE LIMITED TO PLUS OR MINUS FIFTEEN PERCENT PER YEAR UNLESS A CONSENSUS OVERRIDE IS OBTAINED."

"Okay, then cut the allocation fifteen percent for each year for the next five years. And increase the allocation for peas by the same amount.

"YOU REQUEST HAS BEEN ANALYZED. PREDICTED RETAIL PRICES OF SPINACH AND PEAS FOR NEXT FIVE YEARS ARE DISPLAYED ON SCREEN A. DO YOU WISH TO MODIFY THE MASTER PLANNING FILE?"

"Hey, Harry, look at that. In three years spinach will be twelve dollars a pound and peas will only cost twenty cents!"

"Socrat, please modify the files."

"Harry, look at the monitor! Isn't that your Dad coming out of his office?"

"Right! Quick, Spike, tear that paper out of the terminal. Socrat, log us off right away!"

"Here he comes, Harry."

"Hey, you kids aren't supposed to be in here."

"I'm sorry, Dad. I was just showing Spike the computer."

"You didn't touch anything, did you?"

"I just tried to type some stuff on the terminal."

"I guess that couldn't have hurt anything. You see, this computer has built-in security checks. You know what those are, Spike?"

"I don't think so, Mr. Pembroke."

"Well, suppose someone wanted to get access to the computer to find out some important things that are stored inside or even to change around some of those things. He would have to know a logon name first and then he would have to know a secret password. And those passwords are changed every month. So not just anyone could come in here and use the computer. You understand that?"

"I guess so, Mr. Pembroke."

"Hey, Dad, can we come down and visit your office again next week?"

The Boy Who Predicted Earthquakes

MARGARET ST. CLAIR

"Naturally, you're skeptical," Wellman said. He poured water from a carafe, put a pill on his tongue, washed the pill down. "Naturally, understandably. I don't blame you, wouldn't dream of blaming you. A good many of us here at the studio had your attitude, I'm afraid, when we started programming this boy Herbert. I don't mind telling you, just between ourselves, that I myself was pretty doubtful that a show of that sort would be good television."

Wellman scratched behind an ear while Read looked on with scientific interest. "Well, I was wrong," Wellman said, putting the hand down again. "I'm pleased to say that I was 1,000 percent wrong. The kid's first, unannounced, unadvertised show brought nearly 1,400 pieces of mail. And his rating nowadays . . ." He leaned toward Read and whispered a figure.

"Oh," Read said.

"We haven't given it out yet, because those buzzards at Purple simply wouldn't believe us. But it's the plain simple truth. There isn't another TV personality today who has the following the kid has. He's on shortwave, too, and people tune him in all over the globe. Every time he has a show the post office has to send two special trucks with his mail. I can't tell you how happy I am, Read, that you scientists are thinking

about making a study of him at last. I'm terrifically sincere about this."

"What's he like personally?" Read asked.

"The kid? Oh, very simple, very quiet, very, very sincere. I like him tremendously. His father—well, he's a real character."

"How does the program work?"

"You mean, how does Herbert do it? Frankly, Read, that's something for you researchers to find out. We haven't the faintest idea of what happens, really.

"I can tell you the program details, of course. The kid has a show twice a week, Mondays and Fridays. He won't use a script"—Wellman grimaced—"which is pretty much a head-ache for us. He says a script dries him up. He's on the air for twelve minutes. Most of that time he just talks, telling the viewers about what he's been doing in school, the books he's been reading, and so on. The kind of stuff you'd hear from any nice, quiet boy. But he always makes one or two predictions, always at least one, and never more than three. They are always things that will happen within forty-eight hours. Herbert says he can't see any farther ahead than that."

"And they do happen?" Read said. It was less a question than a statement.

"They do," Wellman replied, somewhat heavily. He puffed out his lips. "Herbert predicted the stratosphere liner wreck off Guam last April, the Gulf States hurricane, the election results. He predicted the submarine disaster in the Tortugas. Do you realize that the FBI has an agent sitting in the studio with him during every show out of range of the scanners? That's so he can be taken off the air immediately if he says anything that might be contrary to public policy. They take him that seriously.

"I went over the kid's record yesterday when I heard the University was thinking of studying him. His show has been going out now for a year and a half, twice a week. He's made 106 predictions during that time. And every one of them, every single one of them, has come true. By now the general public has such confidence in him that"—Wellman licked his lips and hunted for a comparison—"that they'd believe him if he predicted the end of the world or the winner of the Irish Sweepstakes.

"I'm sincere about this, Read, terrifically sincere. Herbert is the biggest thing in TV since the invention of the selenium cell. You can't overestimate him or his importance. And now, shall we go take in his show? It's just about time for him to go on."

Wellman got up from his desk chair, smoothing the design of pink and purple penguins on his necktie into place. He led Read through the corridors of the station to the observation room of studio 8G, where Herbert Pinner was.

Herbert looked, Read thought, like a nice, quiet boy. He was about fifteen, tall for his age, with a pleasant, intelligent, somewhat careworn face. He went about the preparation for his show with perfect composure which might hide a touch of distaste.

". . . I have been reading a very interesting book," Herbert said to the TV audience. "Its name is *The Count of Monte Cristo.* I think almost anybody might enjoy it." He held up the book for the viewers to see. "I have also begun a book on astronomy by a man named Duncan. Reading that book has made me want a telescope. My father says that if I work hard and get good grades in school, I can have a small telescope at the end of the term. I will tell you what I can see with the telescope after we buy it.

"There will be an earthquake, not a bad one, in the north Atlantic States tonight. There will be considerable property damage, but no one will be killed. Tomorrow morning about ten o'clock they will find Gwendolyn Box, who has been lost in the Sierras since Thursday. Her leg is broken but she will still be alive.

"After I get the telescope I hope to become a member of the society of variable star observers. Variable stars are stars whose brightness varies either because of internal changes or because of external causes . . ."

At the end of the program Read was introduced to young Pinner. He found the boy polite and cooperative, but a little remote.

"I don't know just how I do it, Mr. Read," Herbert said when a number of preliminary questions had been put to him. "It isn't pictures, the way you suggested, and it isn't words. It's just—it just comes into my mind.

"One thing I've noticed is that I can't predict anything unless I more or less know what it is. I could predict about the earthquake because everyone knows what a quake is, pretty much. But I couldn't have predicted about Gwendolyn Box if I hadn't known she was missing. I'd just have had a feeling that somebody or something was going to be found."

"You mean you can't make predictions about anything unless it's in your consciousness previously?" Read asked intently.

Herbert hesitated. "I guess so," he said. "It makes a . . . a spot in my mind, but I can't identify it. It's like looking at a light with your eyes shut. You know a light is there, but that's all you know about it. That's the reason why I read so many books. The more things I know about, the more things I can predict.

"Sometimes I miss important things, too. I don't know why that is. There was the time the atomic pile exploded and so many people were killed. All I had for that day was an increase in employment.

"I don't know how it works, really, Mr. Read. I just know it does."

Herbert's father came up. He was a small, bouncing man with the extrovert's persuasive personality. "So you're going to investigate Herbie, hum?" he said when the introductions had been performed. "Well, that's fine. It's time he was investigated."

"I believe we are," Read answered with a touch of caution. "I'll have to have the appropriation for the project approved first."

Mr. Pinner looked at him shrewdly. "You want to see whether there's an earthquake first, isn't that it? It's different when you hear him saying it himself. Well, there will be. It's a terrible thing, an earthquake." He clicked his tongue deprecatingly. "But nobody will be killed, that's one good thing. And they'll find that Miss Box the way Herbie says they will."

The earthquake arrived about 9:15, when Read was sitting under the bridge lamp reading a report from the Society for Psychical Research. There was an ominous muttering rumble and then a long, swaying, seasick roll.

Next morning Read had his secretary put through a call to

Haffner, a seismologist with whom he had a casual acquaintanceship. Haffner, over the phone, was definite and brusque.

"Certainly there's no way of foretelling a quake," he snapped. "Not even an hour in advance. If there were, we'd issue warnings and get people out in time. There'd never be any loss of life. We can tell in a general way where a quake is likely, yes. We've known for years that this area was in for one. But as for setting the exact time—you might as well ask an astonomer to predict a nova for you. He doesn't know, and neither do we. What brought this up, anyway? The prediction made by that Pinner kid?"

"Yes. We're thinking of observing him."

"Thinking of it? You mean you're only just now getting around to him? Lord, what ivory towers you research psychologists must live in!"

"You think he's genuine?"

"The answer is an unqualified yes."

Read hung up. When he went out to lunch he saw by the headlines that Miss Box had been found as Herbert had predicted on his TV program.

Still he hesitated. It was not until Thursday that he realized that he was hesitating not because he was afraid of wasting the university's money on a fake, but because he was all too sure that Herbert Pinner was genuine. He didn't at bottom want to start this study. He was afraid.

The realization shocked him. He got the dean on the phone at once, asked for his appropriation, and was told there would be no difficulty about it. Friday morning he selected his two assistants for the project, and by the time Herbert's program was nearly due to go out, they were at the station.

They found Herbert sitting tensely on a chair in studio 8G with Wellman and five or six other station executives clustered around him. His father was dancing around excitedly, wringing his hands. Even the FBI man had abandoned his usual detachment and impassivity, and was joining warmly in the argument. And Herbert, in the middle, was shaking his head and saying, "No, no, I can't," over and over again doggedly.

"But why not, Herbie?" his father wailed. "Please tell me why not. Why won't you give your show?"

"I can't," Herbie said. "Please don't ask me. I just can't." Read noticed how white the boy was around the mouth.

"But Herbie, you can have anything you want, anything, if you only will! That telescope—I'll buy it for you tomorrow. I'll buy it tonight!"

"I don't want a telescope," young Pinner said wanly. "I don't want to look through it."

"I'll get you a pony, a motorboat, a swimming pool! Herbie, I'll get you anything!"

"No," Herbert said.

Mr. Pinner looked around him desperately. His eyes fell on Read, standing in the corner, and he hurried over to him. "See what you can do with him, Mr. Read," he panted.

Read chewed his lower lip. In a sense it was his business. He pushed his way through the crowd to Herbert, and put his hand on his shoulder. "What's this I hear about you not wanting to give your show today, Herbert?" he asked.

Herbert looked up at him. The harassed expression in his eyes made Read feel guilty and contrite. "I just can't," he said. "Don't you start asking me too, Mr. Read."

Once more Read chewed his lip. Part of the technique of parapsychology lies in getting subjects to cooperate. "If you don't go on the air, Herbert," he said, "a lot of people are going to be disappointed."

Herbert's face took on a tinge of sullenness. "I can't help it," he said.

"More than that, a lot of people are going to be frightened. They won't know why you aren't going on the air, and they'll imagine things. All sorts of things. If they don't view you an awful lot of people are going to be scared."

"I—" Herbert said. He rubbed his cheek. "Maybe that's right," he answered slowly. "Only . . ."

"You've got to go on with your show."

Herbert capitulated suddenly. "All right," he said, "I'll try."

Everyone in the studio sighed deeply. There was a general motion toward the door of the observation room. Voices were raised in high-pitched, rather nervous chatter. The crisis was over, the worst would not occur.

The first part of Herbert's show was much like the others had been. The boy's voice was a trifle unsteady and his hands had a tendency to shake, but these abnormalities would have passed the average viewer unnoticed. When perhaps five minutes of the show had gone, Herbert put aside the books and drawings (he had been discussing mechanical drawing) he had been showing his audience, and began to speak with great seriousness.

"I want to tell you about tomorrow," he said. "Tomorrow"— he stopped and swallowed— "tomorrow is going to be different from what anything in the past has been. Tomorrow is going to be the start of a new and better world for all of us."

Read, listening in the glass-enclosed room, felt an incredulous thrill race over him at the words. He glanced around at the faces of the others and saw that they were listening intently, their faces strained and rapt. Wellman's lower jaw dropped a little, and he absently fingered the unicorns on his tie.

"In the past," young Pinner said, "we've had a pretty bad time. We've had wars—so many wars—and famines and pestilences. We've had depressions and haven't known what caused them, we've had people starving when there was food and dying of diseases for which we knew the cure. We've seen the wealth of the world wasted shamelessly, the rivers running black with the washed-off soil, while hunger for all of us got surer and nearer every day. We've suffered, we've had a hard time.

"Beginning tomorrow"—his voice grew louder and more deep—"all that is going to be changed. There won't be any more wars. We're going to live side by side like brothers. We're going to forget about killing and breaking and bombs. From pole to pole the world will be one great garden, full of richness and fruit, and it will be for all of us to have and use and enjoy. People will live a long time and live happily, and when they die it will be from old age. Nobody will be afraid any more. For the first time since human beings lived on earth, we're going to live the way human beings should.

"The cities will be full of the richness of culture, full of art

and music and books. And every race on earth will contribute to that culture, each in its degree. We're going to be wiser and happier and richer than any people have ever been. And pretty soon"—he hesitated for a moment, as if his thought had stumbled—"pretty soon we're going to send out rocket ships.

"We'll go to Mars and Venus and Jupiter. We'll go to the limits of our solar system to see what Uranus and Pluto are like. And maybe from there—it's possible—we'll go on and visit the stars.

"Tomorrow is going to be the beginning of all that. That's all for now. Good-by. Good night."

For a moment after he had ceased no one moved or spoke. Then voices began to babble deliriously. Read, glancing around, noticed how white their faces were and how dilated their eyes.

"Wonder what effect the new setup will have on TV?" Wellman said, as if to himself. His tie was flopping wildly about. "There'll be TV, that's certain—it's part of the good life." And then, to Pinner, who was blowing his nose and wiping his eyes, "Get him out of here, Pinner, right away. He'll be mobbed if he stays here."

Herbert's father nodded. He dashed into the studio after Herbert, who was already surrounded, and came back with him. With Read running interference, they fought their way through the corridor and down to the street level at the station's back.

Read got into the car uninvited and sat down opposite Herbert on one of the folding seats. The boy looked quite exhausted, but his lips wore a faint smile. "You'd better have the chauffeur take you to some quiet hotel," Read said to the senior Pinner. "You'd be beseiged if you went to your usual place."

Pinner nodded. "Hotel Triller," he said to the driver of the car. "Go slowly, driver. We want to think."

He slipped his arm around his son and hugged him. His eyes were shining. "I'm proud of you, Herbie," he declared solemnly, "as proud as can be. What you said—those were wonderful, wonderful things."

The driver had made no move to start the car. Now he

turned round and spoke. "It's young Mr. Pinner, isn't it? I was watching you just now. Could I shake your hand?"

After a moment Herbert leaned forward and extended it. The chauffeur accepted it almost reverently. "I just want to thank you—just want to thank you— Excuse me, Mr. Herbert. But what you said meant a lot to me. I was in the last war."

The car slid away from the curb. As it moved downtown, Read saw that Pinner's injunction to the driver to go slowly had been unnecessary. People were thronging the streets already. The sidewalks were choked. People began to spill over onto the pavements. The car slowed to a walk, to a crawl, and still they poured out. Read snapped the blinds down for fear Herbert should be recognized.

Newsboys were screaming on the corners in raucous hysteria. As the car came to a halt Pinner opened the door and slipped out. He came scrambling back with an armload of papers he had bought.

"NEW WORLD COMING!" one read, another "MILLENNIUM TOMORROW!" and another quite simply, "JOY TO THE WORLD!" Read spread the papers out and began to read the story in one of them.

"A 15-year-old boy told the world that its troubles were over beginning tomorrow, and the world went wild with joy. The boy, Herbert Pinner, whose uncannily accurate predictions have won him a worldwide following, predicted an era of peace, abundance and prosperity such as the world has never known before. . . ."

"Isn't it wonderful, Herbert?" Pinner panted. His eyes were blazing. He shook Herbert's arm. "Isn't it wonderful? Aren't you glad?"

"Yes," Herbert said.

They got to the hotel at last and registered. They were given a suite on the sixteenth floor. Even at this height they could faintly hear the excitement of the crowd below.

"Lie down and rest, Herbert," Mr. Pinner said. "You look worn out. Telling all that—it was hard on you." He bounced around the room for a moment and then turned to Herbert apologetically. "You'll excuse me if I go out, son, won't you? I'm too excited to be quiet. I want to see what's going on

outside." His hand was on the knob of the door.

"Yes, go ahead," Herbert answered. He had sunk down in a chair.

Read and Herbert were alone in the room. There was silence for a moment. Herbert laced his fingers over his forehead and sighed.

"Herbert," Read said softly, "I thought you couldn't see into the future for more than forty-eight hours ahead."

"That's right," Herbert replied without looking up.

"Then how could you foresee all the things you predicted tonight?"

The question seemed to sink into the silence of the room like a stone dropped into a pond. Ripples spread out from it. Herbert said, "Do you really want to know?"

For a moment Read had to hunt for the name of the emotion he felt. It was fear. He answered, "Yes."

Herbert got up and went over to the window. He stood looking out, not at the crowded streets, but at the sky—where, thanks to daylight-saving time, a faint sunset glow yet lingered.

"I wouldn't have known if I hadn't read the book," he said, turning around, the words coming out in a rush. "I'd just have known something big—big—was going to happen. But now I know. I read about it in my astronomy book.

"Look over here." He pointed to the west, where the sun had been. "Tomorrow it won't be like this."

"What do you mean?" Read cried. His voice was sharp with anxiety. "What are you trying to say?"

"That . . . tomorrow the sun will be different. Maybe it's better this way. I wanted them to be happy. You mustn't hold it against me, Mr. Read, that I lied to them."

Read turned to him fiercely. "What is it? What's going to happen tomorrow? You've got to say!"

"Why, tomorrow the sun—I've forgotten the word. What is it they call it when a star flares up suddenly, when it becomes a billion times hotter than it was before?"

"A nova?" Read cried.

"That's it. Tomorrow . . . the sun is going to explode."